Palo Alto City Library

The individual borrower is responsible for all library material borrowed on his or her card.

Charges as determined by the CITY OF PALO ALTO will be assessed for each overdue item.

Damaged or non-returned property will be billed to the individual borrower by the CITY OF PALO ALTO.

P.O. Box 10250, Palo Alto, CA 94303

An I Can Read Book®

Wizard and Wart at SEA

story by **Janice Lee Smith**
pictures by **Paul Meisel**

HarperCollins*Publishers*

To William Christopher Martin
and his grandma Liz,
who taught him to love books
—J.L.S.

For Grandma Hortense
—P.M.

HarperCollins®, ®, and I Can Read Book® are trademarks of HarperCollins Publishers Inc.

Wizard and Wart at Sea
Text copyright © 1995 by Janice Lee Smith
Illustrations copyright © 1995 by Paul Meisel
Printed in the U.S.A. All rights reserved.

Library of Congress Cataloging-in-Publication Data
Smith, Janice Lee, date
    Wizard and Wart at sea / story by Janice Lee Smith ; pictures by Paul Meisel.
        p.   cm. — (An I can read book)
    Sequel to: Wizard and Wart
    Summary: While trying to relax on the beach with his dog Wart, Wizard uses his magic to
get rid of pesky seagulls but finds his solution to be just as bad as the original problem.
    ISBN 0-06-024754-1. — ISBN 0-06-024755-X (lib. bdg.)
    [1. Wizards—Fiction.   2. Magic—Fiction.   3. Animals—Fiction.   4. Beaches—Fiction.]
I. Meisel, Paul, ill.   II. Title.   III. Series.
PZ7.S6499Wi   1995   94-3200
[E]—dc20   CIP
                                                                                                  AC

Typography by Alicia Mikles
6   7   8   9   10
❖

Contents

Chapter One

"Wizard work is hard work,"
Wizard told Wart.
"Wart work is even harder,"
said Wart.
"We need a vacation,"
said Wizard.

"Let's go to the sea

where it is nice and quiet.

We can eat and read on the beach,"

said Wizard.

"I will eat on the beach and

tan my tummy," said Wart.

"We're on our way!" said Wizard.

He hocused and pocused.

Poof!

Wizard and Wart were

at a hotel on the beach.

"The hotel is full," said the clerk.

"Everyone is having meetings.

There is a meeting of plumbers.

There is a meeting of pansy potters.

There is a meeting of pickle packers."

"We are a meeting

of Wizard and Wart,"

Wizard said.

"Then you may have a room,"

said the clerk.

The beach was full of pansy potters,
pickle packers, and plumbers.

"This is the life," Wizard said.

"Nothing to do but read."

"And nothing to do but eat,"

said Wart.

Soon Wart fell asleep

and started to snore.

Soon Wizard was snoring too.

Suddenly Wizard heard a scream.

"Help!" yelled Wart.

Seagulls swooped around him.

"Do magic," cried Wart.

"Make them go away!"

"I don't work on vacation,"

said Wizard.

He picked up his book again.

More seagulls came.

They covered every inch of Wart.

"Vacation is vacation,"

said Wizard,

"but enough is enough!"

Wizard hopped and bopped.

"Fish eyes and icky stuff!"

he yelled.

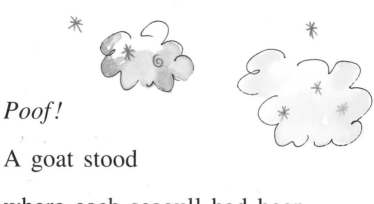

Poof!

A goat stood

where each seagull had been.

"Sorry," Wizard told Wart.

"I should never do magic

in a hurry."

"I don't think they allow

goats at the beach," said Wart.

Chapter Two

There were goats
all over the beach.

Everybody sat in boats

on the sea.

19

"This is the life,"

Wizard said.

Wart ate cookies

and got seasick.

"Do magic," Wart begged.

"Get the goats off the beach

so we can go back there."

"I don't work on vacation,"

said Wizard.

Soon a flock of seagulls landed
on Wart.

"Help!" cried Wart.

"A curse and worse!" yelled Wizard.

"Can't a wizard get a little rest?"

Wizard stomped and stormed.

"Seashells and whale tails!"

he shouted.

Splash!

Wizard fell into the sea.

"Whales?" yelled Wart.

"Why did you change them
into whales?"

"It seemed like a good idea
at the time,"

said Wizard, and sneezed.

25

Chapter Three

The beach was full of goats.

The sea was full of whales.

Everybody crowded
around the hotel pool.

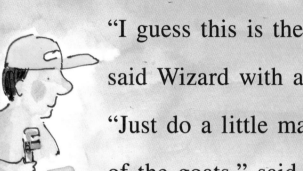

"I guess this is the life,"
said Wizard with a sigh.
"Just do a little magic to get rid
of the goats," said Wart.
"Then we can go to the beach."

"No more magic!" said Wizard.

"I don't work on vacation."

Soon a herd of seagulls

landed on Wart.

"Wait!" Wart shouted at Wizard,

but it was too late.

Wizard was already

fussing and fuming.

"Bat wings and monkey swings!"

he shouted.

Poof!

Then there were monkeys
where seagulls had been.

"You are rotten guests!"

the hotel clerk yelled.

"It is bad manners

to throw magic spells around."

"No one can go on the beach

because of the goats,"

said the plumbers.

"No one can go in the sea

because of the whales,"

said the pansy potters.

"Now no one can swim in the pool

because of the monkeys!"

said the pickle packers.

"My goodness!" said Wizard.

"You all look terrible.

You need a vacation."

"Do something!"

yelled the hotel clerk.

Chapter Four

"Vacation's over," Wizard said.

"Make room for magic!"

Wizard razzled and dazzled.

"Oh!" said the guests. "Ah!"

"Good grief," said Wart.

"We can't go wrong

with birds of song," sang Wizard.

Poof!

The whales, goats, and monkeys

were gone.

Songbirds filled the sky.

"This is wonderful!"

said the potters, packers,

and plumbers.

"Come back anytime,"

said the hotel clerk.

Then he remembered

the goats.

"On second thought,

just keep in touch."

Then he remembered

the whales and monkeys.

"On last thought, just go away."

"It is time to go home," said Wizard.

"I am tired of sand, sea, and sun."

Wizard hopped and bopped.

Poof!

At home

Wizard settled down with his book.

Wart had a snack,

and soon he was snoring.

"This is the life," said Wizard.

And then he was snoring too.